Billy *and the* Big New School

For Brodie

Anholt, Laurence.
Billy and the big new school /
pictures by Catherine Anholt; story by Laurence Anholt.
p. cm.
Summary: Billy is nervous about starting school,
but as he cares for a sparrow that eventually learns to fly on its own,
he realizes that he too can look after himself.
ISBN 0-8075-0743-1
[1. First day of school—Fiction. 2. Schools—Fiction. 3. Birds—Fiction.]
I. Anholt, Catherine, ill. II. Title.
PZ7.A58635Bi 1999 [E]—dc21 98-39774
CIP
AC

Originally published in the United Kingdom by Orchard Books,
an imprint of the Watts Publishing Group, London.

Text © 1997 Laurence Anholt
Illustrations © 1997 Catherine Anholt
Published in 1999 by Albert Whitman & Company,
6340 Oakton Street, Morton Grove, Illinois 60053-2723.
Published simultaneously in Canada by
General Publishing, Limited, Toronto.
Printed in Singapore
10 9 8 7 6 5 4 3 2

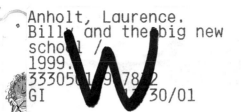

Billy *and the* Big New School

Pictures by Catherine Anholt
Story by Laurence Anholt

Albert Whitman & Company • Morton Grove, Illinois

Billy was starting at a new school.

It was very exciting, but it made him feel a little funny inside.

On the Sunday before he started, Billy didn't want any breakfast at all. He kept thinking about that great big school and all the great big children.

Billy began to wish that he could stay at home with his mom.

"You're just like a little bird who doesn't want to leave his nest," said Billy's mom, giving him a hug.

Billy took the rest of his breakfast out to the bird feeder and
waited for the birds, who were his friends. The birds weren't
scared of Billy because he was small like them, and he knew how
to stand very still.

Billy knew all the different birds. He had made pictures of them
for the kitchen walls. His mom had helped him write their names.

blackbird

starling

pigeon

thrush

sparrow

That Sunday morning, Billy talked to the birds.
He told them about the new school.

He told them he was worried that he would get lost…

or start to cry.

He told the birds that his mom had bought him new shoes with laces that were hard to tie.

"I wish I was a bird," said Billy. "Then I wouldn't have to worry about school at all. Or shoelaces."

Suddenly, the birds started making a terrible noise. Billy saw a new bird sitting on the ground. It was a tiny sparrow. All the other birds were picking on it and trying to chase it away.

But the little sparrow couldn't fly well. It wasn't really ready to take care of itself.

It was the smallest, grubbiest, weediest, most dusty bird Billy
had ever seen. Billy called his mom.

Billy's mom ran out and chased the other birds away. Then
they carried the little sparrow inside.

The kitchen was warm, but
the sparrow was shivering.
Billy found the box from his
new shoes.

He made a bed of cotton balls
and put the bird gently inside.
He could feel its little heart
beating.

Then Billy gave the bird a bowl
of water and a tiny piece of
bread. But it wasn't hungry.

So Billy sat and talked gently
to the sparrow.

All that Sunday, the sparrow sat in the box and watched Billy with a big round eye.

And all that same Sunday, Billy's mom got things ready
for his first day at the new school.

She wrote his name—*Billy*—on his clothes…   his schoolbag…

his pencil case…   and the new shoes with the difficult laces.

That night, Billy had a scary dream. He dreamed that
he was a little bird who couldn't fly, and the other birds
were picking on him.

Then his mom came into the bedroom and gave
him a big hug. And Billy felt better.

In the morning, Billy woke up so early for school that it was still dark.

He had forgotten all about the little
sparrow until he walked into the kitchen and
saw it sitting in the middle of the floor. It had
hopped out of the shoebox, all by itself.

"It must be feeling better," said Billy's mom.
"I think it's time to let it go."
The bird had to go into the big world—
just like Billy.

So Billy gently picked up the little bird and opened the window.

"You have to fly away," he whispered. "You have to learn to take care of yourself—like me."

The little bird looked up at Billy. It seemed to understand. Then it hopped onto the windowsill and flew away into the sky.

After breakfast, Billy took his new schoolbag,
and his mom helped him with his shoelaces.

Then it was time for school.

Billy's teacher was called Mrs. Berry. She was very nice.

She showed Billy where to hang his coat…

and where the toilets were…

and the sink to wash his hands…

and the paints…

and the computer…

and the playhouse…

and the reading corner. Billy even found a big book all about birds.

Some other children were new, too.

Soon another boy came and looked at the
bird book with Billy. Then Billy had a friend.
After lunch, Mrs. Berry talked with the class
about animals. She asked if anyone had a pet.

Daisy had a dog.

Callum had a cat.

Jeremy had a gerbil.

Wendy had a worm.

Tom and Maddy, the twins, had a turtle.
Billy was very interested.

"What about you, Billy?" asked Mrs. Berry.

Billy thought for a moment. Then slowly he stood up.

In a soft voice, he began to tell everyone all about his bird feeder. Then he told them about the poor little sparrow. And about how he had put it in a shoebox until it was ready to fly.

When he'd finished the story, Mrs. Berry began to clap.
And so did all the children in Billy's class. Then Billy sat down.
He knew his face was bright red. But his smile was the biggest
in the school.

That night, Billy had another dream. But this one wasn't scary at all. He dreamed he could fly over the house, over the garden, over the town, and way over the big school, just like a bird. Billy and the birds flew high above the world and turned somersaults over the moon.

A few days later, Billy brought his new friend home from school.

They rolled around in the yard and got all dirty.
But Billy's mom didn't mind.

Billy and his friend had a picnic. They were very hungry.
All the birds came looking for crumbs.

Billy saw one bird that looked almost exactly like the sparrow
from the shoebox. But he couldn't be quite sure, because this
sparrow was bigger, and this sparrow was braver, and this sparrow
was happier, and this sparrow had lots of friends...

JUST LIKE BILLY.